The World of Fashion

Fashion DESIGN

The Art of Style

by Jen Jones

Consultant: Cherie Bodenstab
Assistant Department Chairperson
Fashion Design Department
The Fashion Institute of Design & Merchandising
Los Angeles, California

Capstone press

Mankato, Minnesota

Snap Books are published by Capstone Press,
151 Good Counsel Drive, P.O. Box 669, Mankato, Minnesota 56002.
www.capstonepress.com

Library of Congress Cataloging-in-Publication Data

Jones, Jen, 1976–

Fashion design: the art of style / by Jen Jones.

p. cm.—(Snap books. The world of fashion)

Summary: "Focuses on fashion design from idea to the retail
store"—Provided by publisher.

Includes bibliographical references and index.

ISBN-13: 978-0-7368-6827-3 (hardcover)

ISBN-10: 0-7368-6827-5 (hardcover)

ISBN-13: 978-0-7368-7881-4 (softcover pbk.)

ISBN-10: 0-7368-7881-5 (softcover pbk.)

1. Fashion design—Vocational guidance—Juvenile literature.
2. Fashion designers—Juvenile literature. I. Title. II. Series.

TT507.J666 2007

746.9'2—dc22   2006021866

Editor: Amber Bannerman

Designer: Juliette Peters

Photo Researcher: Charlene Deyle

Photo Credits:
© 2006 Kenpo, Inc., 27 (all); Corbis/Andreea Angelescu, 23; Corbis/dpa/Maurizio Gambarini, 25 (right);
Corbis/Gareth Brown, 13; Corbis/Jose Luis Pelaez, Inc., 8; Corbis/Reuters/Kin Cheung, 14; Corbis/Reuters/Seth Wenig,
24 (left); Corbis/ZUMA/Nancy Kaszerman, 25 (left); Getty Images Inc./AFP/Ammar Abed Rabbo, 21; Getty Images Inc./
Evan Agostini, 24 (right); Getty Images Inc./The Image Bank/Ghislain & Marie David de Lossy, 5; Getty Images Inc./The
Image Bank/Romilly Lockyer, 7, 10; Getty Images Inc./Photonica/Silvia Otte, 17 (middle); Getty Images Inc./Reportage/Joe
McNally, cover (left); Getty Images Inc./Stephen Chernin, 17 (bottom); Getty Images Inc./Stone/Roger Tully, 11; Getty
Images Inc./Taxi Japan/Yo Oura, 17 (top); iStockphoto Inc./Fotostudio/Franz Pfluegl, 15; Michele Torma Lee, 32; PhotoEdit
Inc./Michael Newman, 29; Shutterstock/Anton Oparin, 19; Shutterstock/Cindy Hughes, 9; Shutterstock/Darla Hallmark,
28; Shutterstock/Elena Zarino, 22; Shutterstock/Farsad-Behzad Ghafarian, 12; Shutterstock/Gina Smith, 6; Shutterstock/
malle, 18; Shutterstock/Michelle D. Milliman, cover (right); WireImage.com/Denise Truscello, 16

1 2 3 4 5 6 12 11 10 09 08 07

Table of Contents

Designing Your Future

Take a shopping trip and you're bound to find plenty of super-cute clothes. But have you ever thought about the brains behind them? Fashion designers are the starting point for all of the clothing on the racks. They even design things like swimsuits, jewelry, and shoes. Though the end products can be quite different, the passion behind them remains the same.

This book gives you a firsthand look at the fashion design journey. It starts with the designer's brainstorm and ends on the retail floor. This book will also help you decide whether a future in the fab world of fashion design is for you!

Chapter One

Behind the Seams: The Design Process

Fashion designers aren't just artists. They're creators. Designers brainstorm for new ideas every day. In order to keep fresh ideas coming, designers look for inspiration. Some designers build collages from pictures or fabric samples. Clothing can also be inspired by music or movies.

Fashion is a cycle. In other words, trends that were popular many years ago often come back in style. Designers often look to the past. They come up with new twists on old favorites.

Once an idea is born, a designer creates a sketch. Many sketches are made, but not all of them see the light of day. Only about half of the sketched ideas continue on to design development.

Making the Cut

After a sketch is drawn up as a blueprint, what comes next? A designer makes a pattern and garment sample of her idea. She starts by cutting and draping fabric around a dress form. This shows how the piece will look on a person. Many designers use muslin fabric for draping because it is cheap and flexible.

If a designer is working for a large company, her designs could become part of a clothing line. To make it that far, they must survive a review process. A review team works together to decide whether an idea fits the planned theme. If everything falls into place, the original design is suited for success!

Meet the Review Team Members

The **head production pattern maker** gives input on what it will take to mass-produce the design.

The **head production manager** looks at the costs and materials involved for the proposed garment.

The **merchandise manager** decides if the idea makes sense with current trends and market figures.

Company managers discuss whether the design is a good fit for the company's image and goals.

Chapter Two

The Journey:
How Clothing Is Mass-Made

Once a designer's creation is set for production, it's time to gather the materials! If you read the label inside any clothing piece, you can see the materials used to make it. Examples include polyester or cotton. These are types of fibers that are turned into textiles, and ultimately, clothing.

Textile designers lay the groundwork for cloth production. It is their job to choose the colors, prints, and textures. The future of fabric lies in their hands!

At textile mills, knitting and weaving machines spin fibers into yarns. The yarns later become fabric. Sometimes fabric is also processed at a finishing mill for dyeing or texturing.

Fashion designers use these fabrics for their original samples. They choose different fabrics based on the way the fabric feels, looks, or drapes.

Test Pattern

Just like recipes are used to cook meals, patterns are used to make clothing. Pattern making is done either by hand or by computer. Along with the fashion designer's original sketch, pattern makers work off a garment specification sheet. This document shares important notes about spacing and stitching.

The old-fashioned way is called flat pattern making. A pattern maker draws the pattern on special paper. She uses basic patterns, or blocks, to speed up the process. For instance, a shirt block could be the starting point for several designs. The difference lies in the added details like collars and buttons.

Once complete, a pattern goes through grading. During this process, pattern graders draw up plans for the garment to be made into different sizes. To cut costs, employees called "marker makers" figure out how patterns can be made without wasting fabric. When the pattern is picture-perfect, the pattern maker uses it to make a sample garment. The designer's idea is one step closer to life!

Garments to Go

After sample garments are built and approved, it's production time! Clothing companies give the manufacturing work to factories. Overseas factories are often used because the costs are cheaper.

Inside the factory, many machines and workers make up the assembly line. Sewing machine operators, cutters, and spreaders are just a few of the hard workers. After assembly, garments are carefully checked for quality. If given the green light, they are packed and shipped to distribution centers. From there, they're sent to the stores we know and love!

Work Watchdogs

Long hours are common for factory workers. Sweatshops are a major industry problem. Sweatshops are unsafe, low-paying workplaces that break labor rules. As a result, companies like Nike and Gap have created codes of conduct to protect factory workers. They hope to improve working conditions. Hats off to companies like them!

Chapter Three

Inside the Retail World

After clothes make it through the factory rounds, they are available for our buying pleasure. There are almost 150,000 clothing stores in the U.S. alone. Everyone from the bargain-bin babe to the fussiest fashion slave is sure to score a great find.

◄ Clothing chains like Aeropostale can be found in many cities and malls. These stores are easily recognized by their matching signs, layouts, and merchandise.

◆ Tiny boutiques are one-of-a-kind. The clothing in boutiques is specially selected. Sometimes it is even handmade by the owner.

Thrift stores offer items that are "new to you." This means they have been worn before. The upside is that designer clothes are priced more cheaply. ➡

◆ Department stores carry all kinds of items. You can find shoes, furniture, or cosmetics. Clothing designers get their own sections in the store. Shoppers in small cities can go to department stores for designer clothes.

It's Showtime

Clothing trade shows help designers' creations make it to the retail floor. At these large events, wheeling and dealing is the name of the game. Fashion buyers and sellers meet on common ground. To get their products noticed, clothing companies set up booths. Retail buyers visit each booth to view the latest offerings. At the famous MAGIC trade show in Las Vegas, more than 3,600 manufacturers join in the fun.

Designers and retail clothing buyers also sniff out new trends at textile and bridal shows. Textile shows give a sneak peek at the latest trends. Designers learn about new fabric textures, prints, and colors. Bridal shows are a sea of the latest wedding fashions.

Chapter Four

Creating the Buzz: People, Places, and Faces

Just like the real world, the fashion world has cliques. Fashion's "in crowd" is an elite group of designers. Their fashion houses are haute couture. To be couture, a fashion house must belong to the Syndical Chamber of Haute Couture in Paris. Currently, just 16 designers have this privilege. Among them are Jean-Paul Gaultier, Elie Saab, and Dominique Sirop.

So what makes couture clothes so special? First of all, these very fancy garments are custom-made. Only high quality materials are used. Because each piece is like no other, couture clothes are extremely expensive. Prices can go from $26,000 to more than $100,000 for just one item.

Elie Saab with models

21

Oh, What a Week!

Imagine seven straight days of style. Fashion Week is a gathering of the industry's finest. The event is held twice a year. Fashion Week happens all over the globe from Australia to Mexico. The most high-profile events are in Paris, New York, and Milan.

During Fashion Week, designers unveil brand-new clothing collections. These debuts often inspire the popular styles for the upcoming season. Decked-out models show off the fab fashions on runways. The shows take place in large tents. Pulsing music and colorful lighting add to the excitement. In the crowd, it's easy to spot celebrities and magazine editors. They all sit in the famed front row. It's the Super Bowl of style!

Designing Women

Meet some of fashion's most forward-thinking females:

Betsey Johnson

This fun-loving designer loves to "think pink!" Her 45 self-named stores are bathed in hot pink. Her crazy, colorful clothing is front and center.

Anna Sui

This daring designer discovered her calling early in life. Sui started making her own clothes at age 4. In 1992, she opened the doors to her first boutique. Her rock-inspired styles are now sold in more than 300 stores.

Donna Karan

Donna Karan started as an assistant to designer Anne Klein. When Klein passed away in 1974, Karan took over her company. Today she runs her own multi-million dollar clothing empire.

Diane von Fürstenberg

Diane von Fürstenberg has a legacy all her own. Her jersey wrap dress made a splash in 1972. Today, it has become a female fashion staple.

Chapter Five

Fast-Forward: The Ever-Changing Industry

In the modern "wired" world, it's only fitting for fashion to get a tech makeover. More designers are using computers instead of drawing by hand. Computers let designers play around with different cuts and colors. They have twice the possibilities in half the time!

"Smart clothes" are another advance on the fashion horizon. The clothing of the future will have lots of funky functions, from sensing temperature changes to making phone calls. One forward-thinking company, Eleksen, makes smart-fabric jackets with iPods built into them. No doubt that's music to the fashion industry's ears. Some clothes even have computers built inside them. Clothes with an IQ—now that's intelligent!

CONNECT

CONTROL

LISTEN

27

Chapter Six

Find Your Flair: Becoming a Style-Setter

Now that you know who designed all those great clothes at the mall, you're ready to join their ranks. So how do you go from wanna-be to the designer you want to be? You may not have professional tools at your fingertips yet. But there are lots of ways to dive into fashion design. Take a sewing class. Give your clothes a makeover—add rhinestones to them or try embroidery. Create a collage that shows off your fashion outlook.

Just like fingerprints, each person has her own unique fashion sense. As a future designer, you can stamp a clothing line with your own personal style. Put that artistic talent to use!

Glossary

blueprint (BLOO-print)—a sketch used as a guide for production

debut (DAY-byoo)—a first showing

dress form (DRESS FORM)—a life-size form that designers use to drape and fit clothing

embroidery (em-BROI-dur-ee)—the process of ornamenting material with needlework

haute couture (OHT koo-TUR)—high-end, one-of-a-kind fashion creations

staple (STAY-puhl)—something that is used or worn by many people

textile (TEK-stile)—fabric or cloth that is created by weaving or knitting

Fast Facts

The first rough sketch in the design process is called the "croquis," which is the French word for beginning.

Bravo's popular reality show *Project Runway* puts the hopes and dreams of beginning fashion designers on the TV map.

In 2003, 19-year-old designer Esteban Cortazar became the youngest designer ever to show at New York Fashion Week.

 Read More

Muehlenhardt, Amy Bailey.
Drawing and Learning about Fashion:
Using Shapes and Lines. Sketch It!
Minneapolis: Picture Window
Books, 2006.

Smith, Nancy, and Lynda Milligan.
The Best of Sewing Machine Fun for
Kids. Denver: Possibilities, 2003.

Wallner, Rosemary. *Fashion*
Designer. Career Exploration.
Mankato, Minn.: Capstone Press, 2001.

Internet Sites

FactHound offers a safe, fun way to find Internet sites related to this book. All of the sites on FactHound have been researched by our staff.

Here's how:
1. Visit *www.facthound.com*
2. Choose your grade level.
3. Type in this book ID **0736868275** for age-appropriate sites. You may also browse subjects by clicking on letters, or by clicking on pictures and words.
4. Click on the **Fetch It** button.

FactHound will fetch the best sites for you!

About the Author

Jen Jones has always been fascinated by fashion—and the evidence can be found in her piles of magazines and overflowing closet! She is a Los Angeles-based writer who has published stories in magazines such as *American Cheerleader*, *Dance Spirit*, *Ohio Today*, and *Pilates Style*. She has also written for E! Online and PBS Kids. Jones has been a Web site producer for *The Jenny Jones Show*, *The Sharon Osbourne Show*, and *The Larry Elder Show*. She's also written books for young girls on cheerleading, knitting, figure skating, and gymnastics.

Index